Dedicated to my family: Lauren – for listening to me ramble on for hou[...] and Josephine – for being my greatest inspiration … R.W.

For my little rainbow family: Tsungirirai for never failing to make ever[...] always making every day more fun … B.R.

To my parents, for helping me along my path, and to Sarah, for making the journey all the more bearable … D.I.

Power Shift Publishing, LLC
PO Box 14131
Cincinnati, OH 45250-0131

Twitter: HenryThomas@HeroicHankBooks
Facebook: The Heroic Hank Books
Instagram: heroic.hank.books

Pssst. Hey, you. You in the red hat. I want to tell you the secret of Roosevelt Elementary, but you have to promise not to tell anyone. Can you keep a secret? Okay. Good. Now listen up.

One of the kids in this very cafeteria isn't just a normal kid – he's actually the world's youngest superhero. While all the other kids at Roosevelt love eating sweets, our hero doesn't. He loves broccoli, carrots, bread crusts and white milk.

Yep, little Henry Thomas has it all figured out. He knows he can trade his sweets to the other kids for the healthy stuff they don't like. This may seem crazy, but Henry knows what he's doing.

Henry gains super powers by eating so much healthy food: X-ray vision from carrots, super strength from broccoli, and all kinds of other incredible powers. Henry is the go-to guy to fix his friends' problems, which brings us to Mrs. Williams' 2nd grade class.

It was just an ordinary Tuesday afternoon at Roosevelt Elementary. Terry had a big problem and knew that only one person could help. Terry snuck over to Henry during free time and whispered as quietly as he could, "I was picking my nose, when all of the sudden I felt a tug. My finger is lost inside my nose!"

"Wait, What!?" Henry exclaimed. He looked at Terry's hand and realized that Terry wasn't kidding. "Do you need me to ask Heroic Hank to find your finger?"

"Please," Terry whimpered. All of the kids knew that the only one that could get in touch with Heroic Hank was Henry.

"No problem," Henry stated confidently. "In the meantime, put this sock puppet on so nobody sees how ridiculous you look." Terry slipped the sock puppet over his hand and felt quite a bit better. "Heroic Hank will meet you on the playground after school," Henry continued. Terry breathed a sigh of relief. He knew that if anybody could help him, Heroic Hank could.

Terry paced back and forth hoping Heroic Hank was on the way. In the distance, he saw what looked like a paper bag and two oven mitts bobbing up and down as they approached. It was our superhero. "I heard you need my help," announced Heroic Hank.

"I do," Terry whined. "I lost my finger inside my nose..."

"Henry told me all about it, and I have a plan," said Heroic Hank. "Hold up a finger and when you hear me holler, put me in your nose." Terry watched as Heroic Hank shrank down to almost nothing and then did as he was told.

And so Heroic Hank set off into the unknown to find the missing finger. Looking around the inside of Terry's nose, he realized how difficult this mission would be. "There are boogers everywhere," Heroic Hank said, shuddering. "I need to pay attention, or I might never get out of here."

As soon as those words were out of his mouth, Heroic Hank tripped and fell into a booger swamp. "Uh oh, this mission just got a lot stickier!" Heroic Hank squirmed and wiggled, but the more he moved the more stuck he became. He knew he had to act fast.

The swampy goo quickly began to rise above his shoulders as he sank deeper and deeper. Heroic Hank realized he was about to be in over his head, and he knew what he had to do. "I better use a super jump to break free!" Without wasting another second, Heroic Hank used his powers to jump out of the swamp.

Heroic Hank started to get the feeling he wasn't alone inside the nose. "Hello?" he called out, "Is anyone there?" Nobody answered. Heroic Hank looked and looked all around, but still did not see another soul. His uneasiness remained as he continued his pursuit of the missing finger... But was he really alone?

That question was soon answered as Heroic Hank came to a large wall surrounding a town made entirely of boogers. Heroic Hank trudged along the outside of the wall for quite some time, but never came across an entrance. "This wall seems to go on forever... and I don't see any way in," said a frustrated Heroic Hank. "I wonder if Terry's finger is on the other side. Maybe if I use my super strength I can smash right through it!"

Heroic Hank gathered his strength and used a power punch to break through the wall. The wall shattered into bits and pieces of every size and shape of booger. Almost immediately, he began to hear what sounded like Terry's voice echoing through the cave around him. Aaaah... Aaaaahh... Aaaaaahhh...

After using his ultra-grip to hang on during the sneeze, Heroic Hank found himself standing alone on the outskirts of Booger Town. "That finger has to be somewhere in here," Heroic Hank thought to himself. "I'll head into town and see what I can find out..." More determined to help Terry than ever, Heroic Hank set off toward the slimy city center.

Heroic Hank wandered through the maze-like streets of Booger Town. He could hear the chatter of the booger citizens bragging and cheering about finally catching the menace. "It's being held in the local jail," a lady whispered proudly to her friend.

Heroic Hank said out loud to himself: "That's where I have to go – that has to be Terry's finger they're talking about." Our superhero raced toward the place where the booger citizens were pointing. He was now almost certain that Terry's finger would soon be found.

Zipping through the streets toward the jail, Heroic Hank saw an orderly crowd starting to form around a large building at the top of the hill. The closer he got to the building, the louder the chatter amongst the booger people became. Finally, Heroic Hank saw the finger locked up behind bars. He walked confidently toward the guards standing in front of the gate. "Excuse me, but that's my friend's finger," explained Heroic Hank politely. "You have no idea what I've been through to find it. Can I please have it back?"

"Pipe down!" thundered one of the guards. "That's not our decision. You need to talk to our boss, The Mayor."

The other guard added: "He's already on his way down here, and he's pretty upset about what you did to our wall."

The Mayor of Booger Town soon arrived, and he did not look happy. Heroic Hank stood up straight and spoke directly to the Mayor. "That's my friend's finger and he really needs it back," Heroic Hank pleaded. "He can't wear a sock puppet forever."

The Mayor looked long and hard into Heroic Hank's paper bag eye holes. "This finger has been coming here and destroying our town every day for years!" bellowed the Mayor. "We had no choice but to take it."

"I understand you're upset, and we're both really sorry for what we've done to the town," Heroic Hank stated. "If he promises to stop putting his finger in here, will you let it go?"

After thinking about the proposal put before him, the Mayor agreed. "I know he has more fingers," the Mayor thought to himself out loud. "Keeping just one finger won't guarantee peace." The Mayor then turned to Heroic Hank and said, "This agreement would treat us both well, but if this or any other finger ever comes back, we'll start keeping them forever!"

The Mayor of Booger Town gathered his breath and hollered out to all the people of his town, "The menace will be released and he shall not return! Release the menace!!!"

Heroic Hank gathered up the finger, said goodbye to his new friends, and then said to the finger, "Let's get out of here before the Mayor changes his mind!" He hurried toward the nose's exit with Terry's finger held above his head. "Hey, Terry! We're coming out!"

Heroic Hank escaped the nose with the missing finger in tow. Once our superhero was back on solid ground, he returned to normal size, and popped Terry's finger back into place. Terry stared with great relief at his hand and all five of its fingers. "Thanks a ton!" Terry said, "I promise this will never happen again."

"I hope not," Heroic Hank stated, "There is a whole town of boogers in your nose. They took your finger and vowed to keep it forever if you don't stop picking your nose."

A strange look spread over Terry's face as he tried to understand what Heroic Hank had just told him. "I don't quite get it, but I'll take your word for it. I will never pick my nose again!"

Heroic Hank chuckled, "See you in school tomorrow... Uh, I mean Henry will see you tomorrow..."

"That was fun," Henry said with a sigh. "A little disgusting... but fun." Henry walked home, already looking forward to his next adventure and a healthy snack of carrot sticks.

Made in the USA
Columbia, SC
24 August 2017